COMPANY'S GOING

WITHDRAWN

COMPANY'S GOING

BY
ARTHUR YORINKS

ILLUSTRATED BY
DAVID SMALL

HYPERION BOOKS FOR CHILDREN

Hyperion Books for Children, 114 Fifth Avenue, New York, New York 10011-5690.

First Edition

1 3 5 7 9 10 8 6 4 2

Printed in Singapore

Book is set in 22-point Nicholas Cochin.

LIBRARY OF CONGRESS CATALOGING-IN-PUBLICATION DATA

Company's going / Arthur Yorinks ; illustrated by David Small.

p. cm.

Summary: After inviting two spacemen to stay for dinner, Shirley and Moe are asked to return

with them to their planet Nextoo to cater their sister's rather large wedding.

ISBN 0-7868-0415-7 (tr.)—ISBN 0-7868-2363-3 (lib.)

[1. Extraterrestrial beings—Fiction. 2. Life on other planets—Fiction.

3. Humorous stories.] I. Small, David, ill. II.Title.

PZ7.Y819 Cq   2001

[Fic]—dc21   99-44240

Visit www.hyperionchildrensbooks.com

For my mother and father
—A.Y.

For Sarah, as always
—D.S.

So later, after a nice dinner at Shirley and
Moe's, after all the soldiers, pilots, Marines,
FBI men, and the cousins had said their good-byes,
the visitors from outer space made a momentous
announcement.

"Moe and Shirley from Earth," they spoke. "We have traveled across the great vast sea of space. Past black holes. Through wormholes. We've seen galaxy after endless galaxy—but those were the best meatballs we've ever tasted!"

"You should taste her pot roast," Moe bragged.

"Humans from Bellmore," the spacemen continued. "We have chosen *you* to cater our sister's wedding."

"Oh!" Shirley exclaimed.

"But, but—" Moe tried to speak.

"We'd be delighted," Shirley said as she served some cold drinks. "And where will the happy occasion take place?" she asked.

"On our new planet," said the spacemen. "The planet Nextoo."

"N-N-Nextoo?" Moe stuttered. "Where's Nextoo?"

Moe looked upset.

"Next to Uranus," they answered.

Moe *was* upset.

"Oh, I love Uranus!" said Shirley. "Not that we've ever been there, but I hear it's very nice."

"Then it's settled," the spacemen declared. "We'll pick you up tomorrow at eight. Thank you, Moe and Shirley."

The two guests made their cheerful farewells and left.

But Moe was not cheerful. Later that night, as Shirley packed his socks and underwear, he fumed. "Shirl, do you know where Uranus *is!*"

"So it's a little far," said Shirley. "You'll take a magazine."

"But *Shirl,* an alien wedding? It could be dangerous!" asserted Moe.

"We survived your cousin Harriet's wedding, didn't we?" Shirley said. "We're going and that's that!"

In the morning, at eight, a flying saucer
landed in Moe and Shirley's backyard. Moe and
Shirley were waiting with twenty-seven suitcases.
"I took a few sweaters, in case it gets chilly at
night," Shirley explained.

Moe and Shirley boarded the saucer and with considerable strain it lifted off toward outer space.

They had barely passed the Moon when Moe asked,
"Are we there yet?"

"We just left," said the spacemen.

"Oh," said Moe. "Well, um, do you have any
peanuts?"

"Moe," Shirley interrupted. "You eat too many nuts. Here, I have tuna fish, a jar of pickles, some potato chips, coleslaw, a piece of chicken, some delicious herring from Murray's—they have the best fish—a meat-loaf sandwich, and cake."

Moe picked at the chicken, but he was not really hungry. He was worried. Very worried.

"Shirl," he spoke up. "What if the aliens don't like us? What if they don't like humans? What if they don't like your noodle pudding!" Moe was beside himself.

The spacemen couldn't help but overhear.

"Moe of Earth," they said. "We assure you. Our people are a gentle, peace-loving race. We get along with everyone. Don't worry. You and Shirley will be welcomed with open arms."

At that, the saucer softly landed and Moe and Shirley exited the ship.

"MARTIANS!" the crowd screamed as they spotted Moe and Shirley. "IT'S AN INVASION! RUN FOR YOUR LIVES!"

"NO! WAIT!" cried the two spacemen. "They're not Martians. They're caterers!"

But it was too late. A nervous uncle fired his ray gun, and Moe and Shirley fell to the ground.

"What—are you nuts!" the spacemen said to Uncle Irving. "They're from Bellmore!"

"So clip my nails," said the uncle. "To me—they looked like Martians."

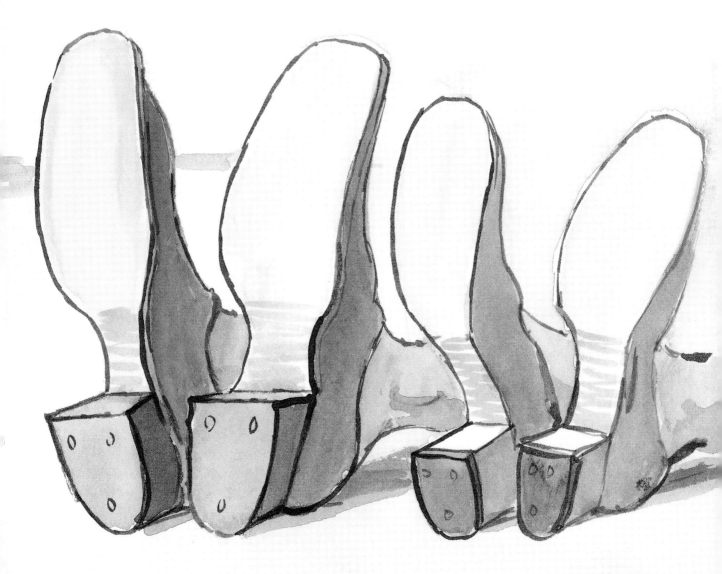

Moe and Shirley were rushed to the hospital, where 492 members of the spacemen's immediate family waited, hoping and praying for their speedy recovery.

"How could Uncle Irving shoot the caterers," sobbed the bride-to-be. "Now what—I have to have a wedding—*with no food?*" she cried.

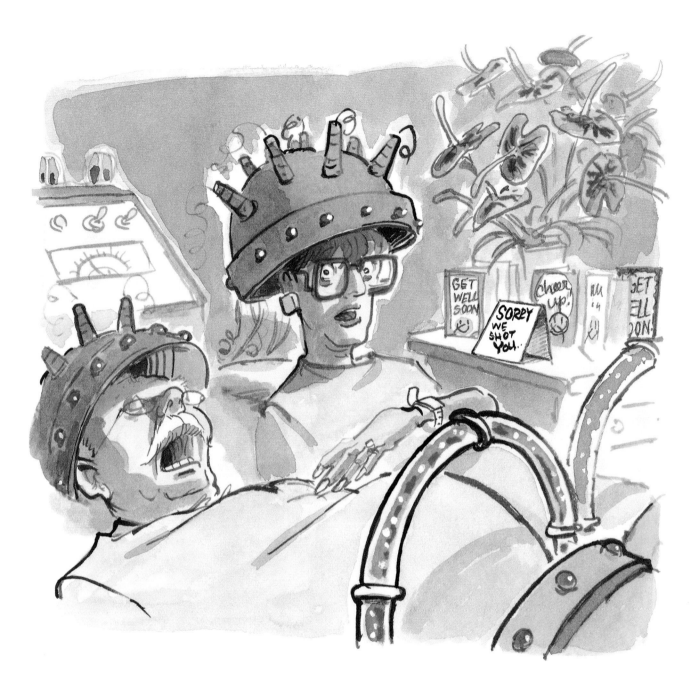

Suddenly Shirley woke up. "No food?" she mumbled. "At a wedding? Moe, wake up!" She gave Moe a nudge. "We have meatballs to make!"

The rays from the ray gun, having cured their arthritis, wore off, and Moe and Shirley went right to work. In one day, Shirley had made so many meatballs it seemed as if there was enough food to feed the whole planet.

And there was. The whole planet came to the wedding.
"We love Shirley's meatballs!" said the happy
spacemen.

Yes, the wedding was beautiful. Moe and
Shirley and the entire population of Nextoo ate
and shmoozed and danced the night away.

The next morning, after breakfast and a little shopping, the spacemen brought Moe and Shirley back to Bellmore.

"So, do me a favor," said Shirley. "Call when you get home, just so I know you got there, and please take a sandwich, it's not good to blast off on an empty stomach."

"We'll miss you," said the spacemen tearfully.

"We'll miss you, too," said Moe and Shirley.

With one last hug, company was gone.

JUN 1 4 2002